When Grampa
Kissed His Elbow

Cynthia DeFelice

Illustrated by Karl Swanson

Macmillan Publishing Company   New York
Maxwell Macmillan Canada   Toronto
Maxwell Macmillan International
New York   Oxford   Singapore   Sydney

Macmillan Publishing Company is part of the
Maxwell Communication Group of Companies.
Macmillan Publishing Company
866 Third Avenue, New York, NY 10022
Maxwell Macmillan Canada, Inc.
1200 Eglinton Avenue East
Suite 200
Don Mills, Ontario M3C 3N1
Printed and bound in Hong Kong   First Edition
10 9 8 7 6 5 4 3 2 1
The text of this book is set in 14 point ITC Zapf International Light.
The illustrations are rendered in acrylics and colored pencil.

Library of Congress Cataloging-in-Publication Data
DeFelice, Cynthia C.
When Grampa kissed his elbow / Cynthia DeFelice ; illustrated
by Karl Swanson. — 1st ed.
p.   cm.
Summary: Maggie's visit to Grampa's house in the country allows
her to see everyday magic like newly hatched mayflies, baby birds,
and ice falling from the summer sky.
ISBN 0-02-726455-6
[1. Grandfathers—Fiction. 2. Country life—Fiction.]
I. Swanson, Karl W., ill. II. Title.
PZ7.D3597Wh   1992
[E]—dc20   90-6696

For Meghan,
whose hair made a home for the wrens,
and
For Mac and Hettie,
who know how to find the magic
—C. D.

To my wife, Erika
—K. S.

"When I was a little girl..." Grampa began.
That was how Grampa always started his stories.

Grampa told me that when he was a little girl, he kissed his elbow and turned into a boy, and he'd been a boy ever since.

Back when Grampa kissed his elbow, exciting things were happening all the time. Strange, wonderful, *magic* things. But I couldn't even kiss my elbow, no matter how hard I tried.

I'd been thinking about it a lot, because I was spending five whole weeks in the country at Grampa's, just Grampa and me.

We were out on the porch. Grampa was cutting my hair with the kitchen scissors, the way he used to cut my mother's hair when summer came.

"When I was a little girl," Grampa continued, "a pixie lived under the porch."

"This porch, Grampa?" I asked.

"Yep," said Grampa, "this very porch."

"Did you see the pixie, Grampa?" I asked.

"I got a glimpse of it from time to time. Not what you'd call a good look, mind you, just a slip of a shadow of a shape. You know, Maggie," he added solemnly, "pixies don't particularly like to be seen."

"I know *I've* never seen one," I said.

"But I knew it was there," Grampa went on.

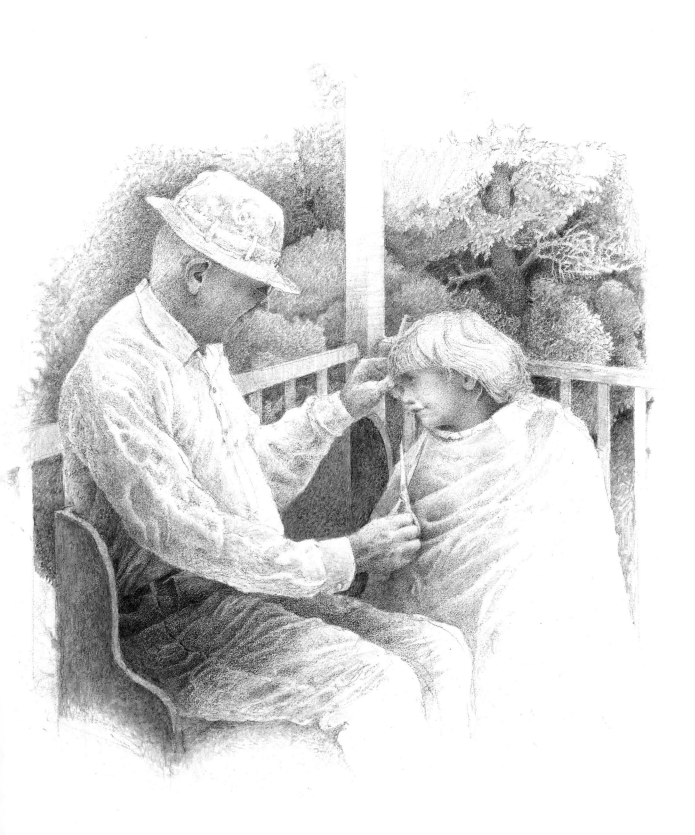

"How did you know, Grampa?" I asked.

"Every night I'd leave a special treat right *there*," said Grampa. He stopped combing and cutting and pointed to the corner of the porch by the rosebush, where two weathered old boards came together.

"What kind of treat did you leave, Grampa?" I asked.

"Oh, some cornbread with strawberry jam, or a piece of fudge, or a biscuit, or maybe something from the garden," answered Grampa, combing and cutting again.

"And what happened?" I asked.

"The next morning the food was gone. The pixie ate it during the night."

"Did you come out to watch the pixie eat?" I asked.

"Of course not," replied Grampa, pretending to sound stern. "I told you pixies don't like to be seen."

"But how do you know the pixie ate it?" I asked. "Maybe it was a dog or a cat or a raccoon."

"No," said Grampa, "it was the pixie."

"How do you *know*?" I asked again.

"Because," said Grampa, and his voice got low and mysterious sounding. "Because every day something good happened to me. Something special. Something magic."

"Every day?" I asked. "Something magic?"

"Yep," said Grampa.

"And the pixie made the magic happen?" I asked.

"That's the way I figured it," answered Grampa.

"I wish magic stuff still happened now," I said as Grampa finished cutting my bangs.

"I reckon it does," he replied.

"I wish the pixie still lived under the porch."
I sighed.

Grampa stood back to inspect his work. "I reckon it might," he said in that same low, mysterious voice.

While Grampa put away the scissors and comb, I got the broom and swept the long, shiny golden strands of my hair off the porch. They blew in the breezes and settled in the grass, or fell softly on the bushes. I thought about what Grampa had told me about the pixie.

That night, before I went to bed, I got the last walnut brownie from the kitchen and went out to the corner of the porch by the rosebush. I moved aside some broken flowerpots and a rusty watering can to make room. In one of the old boards I saw a hole about as big around as a quarter. "Is that where you live?" I whispered. "Down there?"

Back inside, I climbed into the bed that had
belonged to my mother when she was a girl, and
I made a promise: "No peeking till morning."

I left the curtains open so I'd know the minute
the sun came up.

In the morning I ran down the stairs and out
onto the porch. The walnut brownie was gone. I knew
it wasn't a dog or a cat or a raccoon that had eaten
the brownie. It was the pixie. I began to wait for
something good, something special, something magic
to happen.

And before long, something did.

At noon Grampa and I went fishing, but we didn't take a pole. Grampa said he was going to teach me how to tickle a trout.

As we walked to the creek Grampa said, "The fish are resting in the shade near the bank, so we've got to go slow and easy. We don't want to shake the ground or make a shadow on the water."

We tiptoed close to the water, eased down onto
our bellies, and crawled to the edge of the bank. Like
Grampa, I slid my hands down into the cool water
and brought them in slow and easy. The first couple
of times, nothing happened. But then I felt something
cold and wiggly and smooth and slippery against my
fingers. Gently, I tickled my fingers along the fish's
sides until it was still.

Then I lifted it out of the water and onto the grass, where it flashed and sparkled in the sun, silvery green with red and yellow and blue speckles.

Grampa tickled one, too. We cooked them until they were brown and crispy and ate them for supper.

"Tickling trout, that's magic," I said to Grampa.

He agreed. "I reckon so."

That night I left peanut butter cookies on the porch.

The next day, balls of ice bigger than marbles fell from the sky! All of a sudden they came, drumming on the porch roof, clattering on the stone walk, knocking flowers off the peach tree, and bouncing off Grampa's red pickup. Then, just as if somebody had flipped a switch to OFF, they stopped. The whole world was the quietest quiet I'd ever heard.

I scooped up a handful of ice and made a ball. I threw it to Grampa. "Catch!" I called. "It's a magic snowball!"

We played until the sun came out and melted all the hail away.

The day after that, Grampa and I saw thousands and thousands of mayflies hatch. They burst from the water in the creek and flew crazily in the air. We laughed as they flitted and fluttered, jittered and joined. Grampa said they had only one day to live, so they had to make the most of it.

Every night I left a treat for the pixie, and every
day some new magic happened. One night as Grampa
and I lay on our backs in the sweet, tickly grass, a
star went shooting across the sky and disappeared.

"Do you reckon it's the pixie who's making so
much magic?" I asked Grampa.

"I reckon so," he said.

Another night I put out a piece of the strawberry pie Grampa and I had made.

The next morning, as I stepped onto the porch, I saw something I hadn't noticed before. Next to the watering can and the gardening tools and the flowerpots was a pair of Grampa's old leather boots. One boot was filled with small twigs and sticks. Leaning closer, I could see that the twigs had been arranged to make a cup-shaped nest. The nest was lined with strands of something soft and shiny and familiar.

"My hair!" I cried. "Grampa!"

We looked at the little golden nest that held six tiny, white eggs with reddish brown spots. A small, brown bird flew over, perched on the porch rail, cocked her head, and burst into a burbling song. She flew to the nest and, settling her body over the eggs, looked at us as calm as could be.

Grampa and I found the bird book and read all about house wrens.

That night I left a bowl full of the first raspberries of the summer.

When I checked the nest the next day, it held six scrawny babies! Their eyes were closed, but their mouths were wide open! They nestled, safe in Grampa's boot, surrounded by my warm, soft hair.

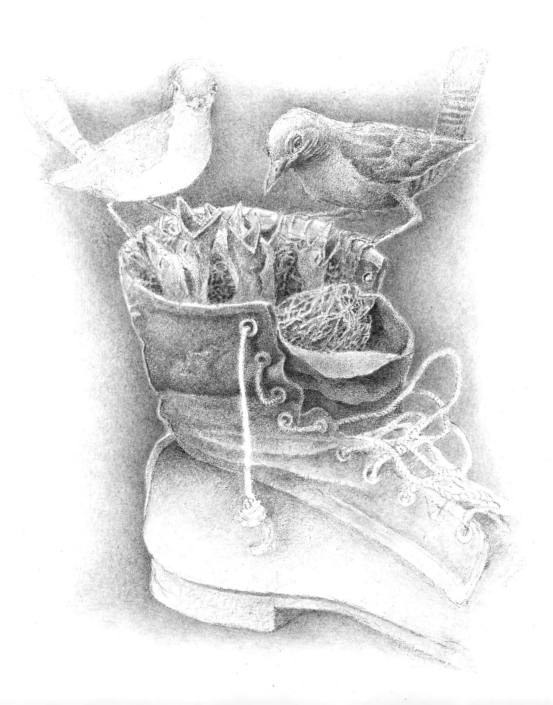

Every night I left another treat for the pixie. And every day the baby birds changed. As their fluffy new feathers grew, they began to look more and more like their parents. The nest could barely hold them.

About two weeks later, Grampa and I got ready to climb into the red pickup and drive to the train station. My visit with Grampa was over.

While Grampa carried my suitcase to the porch, one of the baby birds teetered to the edge of the boot and flew to the porch rail! We held our breaths as, one by one, the other babies tried their wings.

When the nest was empty, I felt sad. It was time for me to go, too.

"Here, Maggie," said Grampa, taking the small, golden nest out of his boot. "The birds don't need it anymore. Take it with you—to remember."

I put the nest in my suitcase.

In my room back at home, I took out the nest and held it and remembered the wrens.

I remembered tickling trout.

I remembered ice falling from the summer sky.

I remembered mayflies dancing the day away.

I remembered a star flying through the night.

I remembered Grampa.

And magic.

I didn't know if there was a pixie under my porch at home. And maybe I couldn't kiss my elbow. But I reckoned there was still some magic left from when my Grampa was a little girl.